MASTER OF THE BEASTS

LUSTOR
THE ACID DART

With special thanks to Troon Harrison

*For my dear nephew, Peter, who writes
amazing stories of his own*

www.beastquest.co.uk

ORCHARD BOOKS
338 Euston Road, London NW1 3BH
Orchard Books Australia
Level 17/207 Kent St, Sydney, NSW 2000

A Paperback Original
First published in Great Britain in 2012

Beast Quest is a registered trademark of Beast Quest Limited
Series created by Beast Quest Limited, London

Text © Beast Quest Limited 2012
Cover and inside illustrations by Steve Sims © Orchard Books 2012

A CIP catalogue record for this book is available from
the British Library.

ISBN 978 1 40831 520 0

1 3 5 7 9 10 8 6 4 2

Printed in China by Imago

The paper and board used in this paperback are natural recyclable
products made from wood grown in sustainable forests. The
manufacturing processes conform to the environmental regulations of
the country of origin.

Orchard Books is a division of Hachette Children's Books,
an Hachette UK company

www.hachette.co.uk

LUSTOR
THE ACID DART

BY ADAM BLADE

ORCHARD

THE ICY

THE NORTHERN
MOUNTAINS

TH

THE FOREST
OF FEAR

WESTERN OCEAN

T

So... You still wish to follow Tom on his Beast Quest.

Turn back now. A great evil lurks beneath Avantia's earth, waiting to arise and conquer the kingdom with violence and rage. Six Beasts with the hearts of Ancient Warriors, at the mercy of the evil wizard, Malvel, who I fear has reached the height of his powers.

War awaits us all.

I beg you, again, close this book and turn away. Evil will rise. Darkness will fall.

Your friend,
Wizard Aduro

PROLOGUE

Sana lurched and almost fell as a shiver ran through the rocky ground. She glanced up at the towering Stonewin volcano. Wisps of smoke trickled from dark cracks in the slopes. *The volcano is speaking!* Sana thought. *I should leave this place before I anger it further.*

With trembling fingers, the medicine woman thrust a last handful of herbs into the sack on her shoulder. On sleek blue wings, a bird with an orange breast swept through the air. It landed on Sana's shoulder with a chirp. The medicine woman smiled. "There you are, Portos," she said fondly. She'd rescued the swallow when it was a scrawny fledgling that had fallen from its nest. Now Portos was her constant companion as she gathered herbs for making healing potions. People from all the northern villages came to Sana for help.

"I didn't get any Tengi Leaf," Sana muttered to the little bird. "And I have none left at home."

Sana craned her neck, staring towards the high craters where the Tengi Leaf grew. Gathering the herb was always risky. As she wondered what to do, another strong tremor quivered through the ground. Small rocks clattered down the slope. Portos flew into the air, shrieking an alarm.

"Let's forget about the Tengi Leaf today," Sana decided. "The volcano is in a dangerous mood."

Turning her back on the craters, she stumbled down the slope with Portos flying overhead. Pools of water, like dark eyes, lay amongst patches of limp grass at the foot of the volcano. The Yellow Marshes. Water bubbled to the surface and steamed. Sana coughed as the acid smell of sulphur burned her throat. This was a dangerous place but Sana had learned a route to cross the marches. Long ago, people had placed stepping-stones in lines like pathways. They seemed to lurk in the dark pools, barely poking above the water. Set one stride apart, the stones were often slippery with moss. Sana picked her way along, balancing from stone to stone.

A tiny wave lapped against the stone where Sana stood. Holding her breath, she scanned the marsh. Suddenly the water surrounding her swirled violently. Portos shrieked and Sana froze. Before her eyes, one of the mossy rocks ahead began to move. It pushed up through the steam, dripping and covered in slimy weeds. A horrible toad-like face, covered in warts, emerged. Then a giant body lurched from the water. Lumps of oozing moss crusted the creature's shoulders, broad chest and dangling arms. It rose to full height, taller than the tallest man that Sana had ever seen. A giant! Water sloshed around its slimy legs as they churned up the mud.

Sana slipped on her stone and one foot touched the steaming water. The creature's misshapen head swivelled towards her. Its eyes were pale and

milky, like those of a dead fish. Its mouth stretched wide open and Sana saw the stumps of rotting teeth and blood oozing from the creature's gums.

"Get away," Sana screamed. "I am a harmless woman. Don't hurt me!"

The Beast's throat began to swell and bulge into a transparent sac bubbling with liquid. Then the swollen sac deflated. Jets of bright yellow liquid flew from the creature's mouth. Sana ducked, throwing her arms up for protection, but drops splattered over her cheeks and arms. Each drop sizzled as it landed, burning her skin. Where the liquid sprayed onto her herb bag, it scorched holes in the fabric. The creature was spraying acid! Panic gripped Sana.

"Help!" she shrieked, but she knew

that she was alone in the marsh.

Sana threw herself towards the next stepping stone but she slipped and plunged into the sulphurous water. Thrashing her feet and arms, she dragged herself to the surface. Her face burned like fire. With a whimper of fear and pain, she pulled herself up the bank. Tears streamed from her eyes as she blundered away from the marsh. Above her, Portos shrieked in distress.

I must get away, Sana thought desperately. Behind her, she could hear the Beast wading through the water. Was it coming after her? Was the sac bulging in its throat again? Sana lurched through the grass, running for her life.

CHAPTER ONE

CURSE OF THE DARK KNIGHTS

"I wish I knew what evil danger we'll face next," Tom said. He frowned, staring at the marble ball that spun between his outstretched hands.

"Isn't the map showing you anything?" asked Elenna.

"Nothing." Tom stared harder at the ball but its surface remained blank in the light of the campfire. The globe had been a gift from the Good Wizard Aduro. On this Quest, it had glowed with paths that had led him to the Knights of Forton – six brave warriors cursed by the Evil Wizard Malvel. The Knights had been summoned from their tombs and now walked again in Avantia. In battle, they had the ability to transform into Beasts they'd once defeated.

But where was the glowing path now? Tom shook his head and placed the globe by his feet, hoping that something would appear soon.

Elenna sat with her legs crossed, whittling something from wood. Nearby, her wolf, Silver, dozed, his pale coat gleaming. Tom's sturdy black stallion, Storm, nibbled at the grass. Beyond them, the Central Plain of Avantia stretched into the darkness.

"I'm worried about the message that Freya sent to Aduro," Tom said.

His mother had said Malvel's anger was growing and that he planned to enter Avantia soon.

Elenna shook her head. "We mustn't think of that," she said. "The Eternal Flame has trapped Malvel in Gorgonia. He can't escape."

"I hope you're right," said Tom with a frown, remembering when he'd forced Malvel into the Eternal Flame where he was now trapped. But for how long? "I wonder what he's planning."

Slumping forwards, he rested his head in his hands. It had only been half a day since he and Elenna had battled with the Black Knight in the mountains and Tom ached with fatigue. The cursed knight had transformed into Shamani the Raging Flame and almost managed to kill the Good Beast Arcta. *How many more of my friends might the Dark Knights threaten?* Tom wondered.

"If I hadn't pushed Malvel into the Eternal Flame, none of this would have happened," he muttered.

Elenna looked up. "Tom!" she protested. "You mustn't blame yourself. You did what you had to by trapping Malvel. We couldn't have known that he would release the Dark Knights. And besides, we've already defeated two of them."

"You're right." Tom took the ball up again. It began to spin in wobbling circles, its surface smooth and blank. Tom's tired eyes stared at it until it was just a blur. The flash of Elenna's knife caught his attention.

"What are you making with that wood?" he asked.

"A flail, like the one used by the Black Knight," said Elenna. "I want to try using one."

"I'll stick with my sword," said Tom.

Suddenly, Silver whined and raised his head.

"He senses something," Elenna said. She laid down the flail and her knife and stared at the spinning ball. Tom

held his breath and leant forwards, his eyes sharp and focused. On the ball's shining surface, a ghostly map of Avantia began to form. A thin line stretched across the map, running eastwards from the Central Plain.

Storm lifted his head from the grass and stepped closer. He laid his warm muzzle on Tom's shoulder and all four of them watched the line heading eastwards.

"It leads to the Stonewin volcano," Tom said. "The home of my old friend, Epos the Flame Bird."

"But which Beast are we fighting?" Elenna asked.

"Lustor," Tom whispered as the name appeared on the map. "There's no time to lose. We can't wait for morning!" He sprang to his feet, slipping the magic ball into Storm's saddlebag and catching Storm's reins in one hand.

Elenna stamped on the embers of the fire and picked up her flail. Together, they mounted Storm as Silver ran in nervous circles. Tom pulled Storm's head around to the east and nudged the stallion into a gallop. Silver raced alongside like a shadow.

As they pounded across the landscape, Tom remembered Aduro's warning: "Be wary," he'd whispered.

But if we don't muster the strength to overcome Lustor, Tom thought, *all of Avantia will be in peril.*

CHAPTER TWO

HUNT OF THE HYENAS

"Good boy!" Tom praised his stallion, leaning forwards to pat Storm's neck.

The Central Plains stretched out into the distance, eerily empty under the moonlight. Only Storm's thundering hooves broke the silence. Silver raced through the waving grass. *I hope we can reach the volcano in time*, Tom thought.

Suddenly the stallion shied

sideways and reared up. Elenna's grip tightened on Tom as they both slipped backwards in the saddle.

"Steady, boy," Tom soothed, gripping the reins firmly with one hand and running the other over the horse's neck.

"What's that?" Elenna asked. She pointed as a small shape flickered past in the darkness.

"Probably just a bat," Tom replied.

The creature flitted overhead again.

"It looks like a swallow," Elenna said. "They used to nest in my village."

To Tom's astonishment, the bird fluttered down and landed in the grass beside Silver. The wolf stared at the bird with bright eyes.

"Silver, stay!" Elenna commanded.

The bird chirped, cocking its head on one side and staring at them. Then it fluttered a few yards away before landing in the grass and calling to them again.

"Maybe it wants us to follow it," Elenna said.

"It could be playing a trick on us," Tom warned. "It might be part of Malvel's plot."

"It's heading eastwards, so we have to follow it anyway," Elenna pointed out.

The swallow rose into the air and soared ahead of them, barely visible against the dusky star-filled sky. Tom squeezed Storm's flanks and they trotted after it.

Mocking laughter drifted in the darkness, raising the hairs on Tom's neck.

"Listen!" he exclaimed, pulling Storm to a halt. "Do you hear that?"

Elenna listened hard. "Hyenas," she said, with a shudder. "They sound as if they're hunting something!"

Storm pawed at the ground. Silver snarled, hackles rising on his back. Cautiously, they advanced towards the high-pitched cries. Soon, Tom could see the gleaming eyes of the pack in the moonlight. Standing in a semi-circle, they surrounded the dark hump of some wounded creature lying on the ground.

"Should we save it?" Elenna asked. But before Tom could reply, the swallow shrieked and chirped loudly, circling above the snapping jaws of the hyenas.

The hump on the ground gave a wordless moan.

"It's a woman!" Tom gasped. He urged Storm forwards, scattering the

hyenas. The woman dragged herself
to her knees, swinging wildly around
her with a walking staff. The hyenas
lunged back at her, avoiding Storm's
lashing hooves. One hyena seemed to
be the pack leader. Larger and more
ferocious than the rest, it had huge
teeth and darker fur. With a snap of its
huge jaws, it sprang at the woman.

"Get away from me, you brute!" she cried, and whacked it across the snout with her stick. Another hyena jumped behind her and tore away a piece of her robe.

Silver darted in, growling and baring his white fangs. He jumped at the hyena's neck and the creature scampered off, still gripping the torn fabric.

Elenna notched an arrow to her bow and let it fly. It hit a hyena's hind leg and the creature gave a screech of pain. Tom swung Storm in closer to the woman and jumped from the saddle, drawing his sword. He rushed at the circle of wild animals, beating them back, step by snarling step. Elenna landed beside him, and whacked a couple of hyenas with the full force of her swinging flail.

The creatures shrieked and fled into the darkness, howling. Storm circled around beside Tom and sent the last hyena flying into the air with a powerful kick. Yelping, it picked itself up and ran after the rest of the pack.

"Here, take my hand," Tom said to the woman. He helped her to stand. She leant heavily on her walking staff as she brushed dirt from her robe. Tom could see that she was shaking. As he peered closer, he noticed that the woman's face was covered in red blotches, like burns, and that her robe and the sack over her shoulder were speckled with scorched holes. Her eyes were swollen closed.

No hyena did this, he thought. *This was the work of something evil.*

CHAPTER THREE

A SAD PARTING

The swallow flew down and landed
on the woman's shoulder. For the
first time, she gave a trembling smile.
"Portos, my faithful friend," she said.
"You brought me help."

"What happened to you?" Elenna
asked.

The woman's face twisted into a
mask of fear. "I am Sana, a medicine
woman," she whispered. "I was near

Stonewin, in the Yellow Marshes picking herbs when something terrible…" Her voice trailed off. She rubbed at her swollen, oozing eyes.

"Something attacked you, didn't it?" Tom asked.

The woman cleared her throat. "A terrible creature – I don't know what it was. It was all slimy and dark. It was huge, taller than three men. It shot acid at me and I fell into the poisoned waters of the marsh."

"Lustor!" Tom and Elenna exclaimed at once.

The magic ball was right, Tom thought, *and the evil Beast is near the Stonewin volcano!*

"We'd better hurry!" Elenna said.

"We can't leave Sana alone here," Tom replied. "We should take you somewhere safe," he said to the medicine woman. "Your injuries need to be treated."

"There's only one cure for this blindness," said Sana, "and that's the blue Tengi Leaf that grows in the Stonewin craters. Alas, I have none of it. I can't ask you to go there and pick any, for it's too dangerous. If we travel east, we'll come to the main northern road. It joins King Hugo's city to the villages of the north. You can leave me there to find my own way home."

Tom glanced across at Elenna and shook his head.

"We can't just leave you," he said. "Come, I'll help you onto my horse. We'll find the Tengi herb for you."

Elenna helped to heave the shaking woman into Storm's saddle. The stallion held perfectly still until Sana was slumped across his back. Tom led the horse onwards.

"What about the Quest?" Elenna muttered as she walked alongside, keeping an arrow notched on her bow in case the hyenas returned.

"We'll just have to go as quickly as we can," Tom said, glancing around for a fresh attack.

"Which won't be that quickly at all," Elenna pointed out. Storm had to walk slowly and carefully, to ensure the injured woman maintained her balance.

Dawn's thin light crept over the eastern horizon as they rode on. The tall grass turned silvery. Soon the sky glowed pink and orange.

Despite himself, impatience gnawed at Tom. *All this time Epos might be in danger!* he thought. Once daylight broke, Lustor would search out the good Beast and attack. Tom only hoped the magnificent Flame Bird could hold Lustor off until he arrived.

"What can you tell us about these Yellow Marshes?" he asked.

Sana groaned softly. "It is a treacherous place," she muttered. "Everything steams and bubbles.

The grass lies dying. The mud is so thick you think you can walk on it. But beware! It will suck you in and swallow you! Horses and dogs and cattle have all been lost in the marshes and never seen again."

"So how do you cross it?" Elenna asked.

"Paths of stepping stones lead in different directions. They are mossy but stable," Sana explained. "They start beneath an old thorn tree burned black by the volcano's heat. But your animals cannot cross. Balancing on the rocks would be too difficult for them."

"We can't leave Storm and Silver!" Elenna cried. "Look, there's a road." Elenna pointed ahead to a pale ribbon of gritty track. "It passes close to the volcano."

"The northern road," Sana said.

Tom scanned the route. It looked passable for him and Elenna, but the surface was far too rough for Storm. Not far away was an empty hut of willow branches. "You can wait safely in that shepherd's hut," Tom told Sana. "We'll leave our animals with you."

Tom helped Sana to dismount, and then led her to the hut. The door hung loose on its hinges, but inside was a pile of old hay.

"You can rest on this," Elenna suggested, leading her to the cushioned spot.

Once Sana was comfortable, Silver lay down beside her to keep watch. "Be careful, young ones," Sana warned Tom and Elenna. "Dark danger lies before you. The volcano is growing restless."

"Don't worry about us. We'll return

soon with the Tengi Leaf to heal
your eyes," Elenna promised.

Tom and Elenna stepped outside.
Tom slipped Storm's saddle off and
slung the saddlebag over his shoulder.
The stallion looked at him in silent
confusion.

"It's all right, boy," Tom said. "We'll
be back soon."

Storm dipped his head and began
to munch at the long grass.

Tom and Elenna strode northwards
as fast as they could go. Dust stung
their eyes. The air, poisoned by the
volcano's fumes, smelled like rotten
eggs. It burned Tom's nostrils and made
him sneeze. The volcano towered
above them, dark and forbidding,
a plume of pale smoke rising from
its peak.

Elenna practised with her flail by

thrashing it against tall plants growing beside the road. "This will be perfect for close combat," she said.

"You'd be safer shooting arrows instead of getting close to an enemy with your flail," said Tom.

Elenna grinned. "Then you get all the glory!"

Tom smiled back and scanned the

sky, searching for any glimpse of the Flame Bird. The road swung close to the base of the volcano and Tom found a flight of crooked steps carved into the crumbling rock. "These must be the steps Sana told us about. They should lead up to the craters," he said. He began to climb with Elenna following close behind. Small earthquakes shivered through the mountain so that it twitched like the skin of a horse throwing off flies. Tom wondered if Lustor's presence had disturbed the region. Although Stonewin had been venting trickles of smoke for many years, there hadn't been a bad eruption within living memory. Epos the Flame Bird usually protected the kingdom from the unpredictable volcano. If it was starting to erupt again, did that mean Epos was in trouble – or worse?

Fear churned in Tom's stomach. Epos must still be alive. He has to be… He couldn't imagine Avantia without his friend. But the volcano looked ready to roar, to belch out fire and ash and smother them. Lava might pour from the smoking craters and wash over nearby villages in a deadly tide. Tom pressed on faster, panting in the heat radiating from the earth.

If Stonewin erupts, we could be killed before we even find Lustor. Then Malvel will win, Tom thought.

"How much higher must we climb to find the Tengi Leaf?" Elenna asked.

"I don't know," Tom replied. "But look, there's a crater beyond that old lava flow. Sana said the herb grows in the craters."

He led the way across the black, bare rock of the hardened lava. It was like a crust of burnt bread. Pieces crunched off beneath Tom's boots, brittle as old bones. When they reached the edge of the weathered crater they saw that clinging to the ridges were clumps of plants with blue leaves shaped like ferns.

"That must be the Tengi Leaf!" Elenna cried. "We'll be able to heal Sana's eyes!"

Tom nodded, studying the crater. Its sides were split with a hundred thin cracks, and hot steam trickled from every one.

"Could you hold the saddlebag while I find a route down?" Tom asked.

He handed the bag to Elenna and stepped forwards, placing his feet slowly and carefully, testing the surface before setting his full weight down. Once or twice, the ground shifted beneath him with ominous creaks. Spurts of steam hissed past his ankles and the rotten smell grew stronger. Far below, Tom could see the orange glow from the crater's deep, fiery heart.

He crouched and stretched out an arm to the Tengi Leaf. The feathery fronds snapped off easily and he passed them to Elenna, who had followed him down. She laid them in Storm's saddlebag, being careful not to crush them.

"Just one more," she said. "That should be en — Tom, look out!"

Tom raised his head as a dark shadow blotted out the sunshine and fell across him.

Something had joined them on the mountain.

CHAPTER FOUR

AN ANCIENT FOE

The Varkule loomed over Tom. Like a giant hyena, it was as tall as Storm and twice as wide, its dark warty skin like burnt leather. Thick bristles of mottled hair crested its spine and drool hung from the tusks jutting from its lower jaw. Its red eyes glittered as it stared at Tom with an expression of malice and cunning. The Knights of Forton had ridden on

Varkules hundreds of years ago and now the Varkules had been liberated from the Tombs, along with the knights, by Malvel's spell.

But where's the knight who rode this creature? Tom wondered.

Tom sprang to his feet, sending pebbles bouncing down into the crater's seething core. He gripped his sword hilt as the Varkule gave a rumbling snarl from deep in its massive chest.

"Elenna, run!" Tom yelled. From the corner of his eye, he saw her bound across the ancient lava flow and then turn, balanced on a ridge.

"Watch out!" she screamed. The Varkule pounced at Tom, its claws whistling through the air. Tom jumped aside but the crumbling surface gave way beneath his foot and he fell sideways. Rolling over, he held his shield aloft and heard the Varkule's claws scratch its surface. Tom leapt to his feet, still holding his shield up, and managed to pull his sword free of its scabbard. He planted his feet firmly and began to beat the Varkule back with long, sweeping slices of his sword. Sparks flashed off the blade as it struck the Varkule's drooling tusks.

Tom fought his way up the side of the crater, over the ridges and the flattened Tengi leaves. The foul stench of the Varkule's breath, like rotting meat, mixed with the sulphur smell of the volcano. Tom gasped for air.

With a sudden lunge, he swung his blade sideways and sliced into one of the Varkule's tusks. It shattered into a splintered stump. The Varkule roared with pain and fury. It swiped Tom's shield aside with its remaining tusk and a huge front paw battered Tom to the ground. Then the Varkule planted its foot on his heaving chest.

"Get off!" Tom spluttered. "Whilst there's blood in my veins, I won't be defeated by you!"

The Varkule leant over him, crushing his ribs with its weight. Black dots filled Tom's eyes and the volcano's peak spun above him as the lack of air made him feel dizzy. He felt the sharp tips of the creature's claws piercing through his tunic one by one. They were like burning needles. Hot spittle fell in strings from the Varkule's jaws as it opened its mouth. Each of its teeth was as large as his fist. Pale slime covered the creature's tongue.

Tom thrashed on the rock but the creature held him down. He tried to yell again at the Varkule but his lungs were collapsing and he could only gasp. *This is the end*, he thought. *It's killing me*. Tom's grip loosened and his sword fell from his hand.

Whoosh–thwack!

The Varkule let out a roar that made Tom's head ring. He saw one of Elenna's arrows jutting from the creature's front paw, which pressed on his chest. Air rushed into Tom's lungs as the deadly grip loosened. Filled with fresh hope, Tom twisted and heaved, freeing himself. He rolled away as the Varkule gnawed at the arrow shaft, snarling horribly. Tom lifted his sword from where it lay on the ground.

As he straightened up, the Varkule used its jaws to tear the arrow shaft from its paw. It sank to its haunches, ready to spring at Tom again. The ground shifted. The cracks in the crater walls began to open wider. Steam hissed from them with the noise of a thousand snakes. Tom staggered, barely keeping his balance,

trying to stay focused on the Varkule.
But there was a worse danger now.
The volcano was finally awakening!

Tom turned to see Elenna
scrambling upwards, her bow slung
over her shoulder. Tom sheathed
his sword and tried to follow. As
the ground shifted again, he threw
himself forwards and gripped the
edge of the crater with both hands.
The rough, ragged rock cut his palms
open and blood ran down his wrists
and arms.

The earthquake's final shudder split
the ground apart in zigzag patterns.
Tom looked over his shoulder and
saw the Varkule stagger first one way,
then the other. Its claws slid across
the lava, leaving long scratch marks.
A crack snaked between its legs and
widened. The Varkule lost its footing

and plunged downhill, bouncing over ridges into the crater's core.

Tom reeled with shock. He fought off a wave of dizziness and waited for the earthquake to subside. Then he hauled himself over the crater's rim and glanced around for Elenna. She was still clinging to the same ridge she'd been on before.

"Tom!" she called and jumped across the rocks towards him. "You beat the Varkule!"

"Thanks to you. You're a fantastic shot," he said. "I hope you're as good with the flail."

"I hope…" Elenna started to reply but then her glance flickered over his shoulder. Her eyes widened in terror. Tom spun around and gazed at the crater that the Varkule had fallen into.

Above the crater's rim rose a glowing red hand. It gripped the crater's edge and clung on. Another hand joined it. The tip of a helmet appeared, then a face covered with a visor, then armour-plated shoulders. With a final rush, a knight hauled himself out of the chasm, clad entirely in brilliant red armour. A fiery glow shimmered from him.

"The Red Knight!" Elenna gasped. "How can he be alive in such heat?"

"Only because of Malvel's evil enchantment," Tom muttered through clenched teeth. "No mortal man could endure it."

The knight pulled his sword from its sheath and held it aloft. The blade shone with white heat like a poker drawn from the fire. Behind the scarlet visor, the knight's eyes were

narrow slits, burning with anger. They swivelled around – and fastened upon Tom. Under that hot gaze, Tom felt himself go cold with dread.

A new enemy had arisen!

CHAPTER FIVE

BATTLE IN THE SMOKE

"You don't need to fight me!" Tom cried to the Red Knight. "You were once a noble warrior, brave and pure of heart. Faithfully, you served the Master of the Beasts with your fellow Knights of Forton. Don't you remember?" If only he could get past the spell Malvel had cast over the knight and persuade him that he was a force for good.

"This isn't going to work," Elenna muttered as the Red Knight scraped his armoured feet across the baking rock.

"Halt!" Tom shouted. "Remember your true character and join with us to fight against evil, as you did long ago!"

Still the knight advanced, glaring. He shimmered in a blur of smoke and heat. Tom squinted into the glare, feeling sweat break out across his skin. He and Elenna backed down the slope. The knight followed, trailing his sword menacingly across the black rock. Sparks flew from the tip.

"What can we do?" Elenna hissed.

We can't even get close with the heat, Tom thought. Then he had an idea. *Or perhaps we can!*

"Crouch down," he said to Elenna
as he lifted his shield overhead.
"Ferno's Dragon Scale might protect
us." Elenna huddled under the
shield's rim and Tom held it steady

against the waves of fiery air.

With a leap, the Red Knight landed before them. The black rock crunched beneath his feet. The knight lifted his blazing sword and Tom braced his arms to receive the blow. The knight's blade smashed across the shield and Tom glimpsed something small and shiny fly off the surface.

"Ferno's scale!" Elenna cried.

Tom squinted as the magic talisman from Ferno flew through the air. It fell amongst the steaming rocks, lost to sight. The knight raised his sword for another swing. Tom and Elenna jumped away, dodging behind a large rock.

"What kind of evil magic are we dealing with?" Tom panted. "No one has ever been able to separate me from the tokens before."

"We have to keep moving!" Elenna cried as the knight stalked them around the rock. The sizzling white tip of his sword whizzed past Tom's ear. He and Elenna scrambled farther down the slope, trying not to trip on the jagged lava. The knight strode after them without pause.

Elenna raised her flail and ran into the knight's path.

"Don't!" Tom shouted. "He's too dangerous!"

But it was too late. Elenna was already swinging her flail at the knight's red helmet. His gauntleted hand shot up and seized hold of it. Instantly the flail burst into flame and crumbled into ash.

Tom jumped forwards, swinging his sword. Its blade rang against the knight's armour, but didn't make

a dent. Scorching heat rushed up the
blade and Tom howled with pain as
the palm of his hand burned. The
smell of hot flesh filled his nose and
he released his grip on the hilt. The
sword skittered over the ground and
onto a slope of loose rock. The blade
rang out as it slid and bounced down
to the bottom of the slope. The knight

pressed forwards, his sword trailing arcs of flame in the air. As they were pushed back, Tom felt his foot slip on a sheet of rock polished smooth by weather and wind. As he fell backwards, Elenna tried to catch him by the arm. His weight over-balanced her and together they tumbled head over heels down the slope.

At the bottom, Tom sat up, his head spinning. Bruises throbbed on his knees and elbows. "Are you hurt?" he asked Elenna.

"Just a few scrapes." She touched her fingertips to a cut on her cheek and wiped away the blood. "Here he comes!"

The Red Knight stamped downhill towards them. The black hole of his mouth opened. Smoke billowed from it as he laughed. Chills ran down

Tom's spine as he glanced around for his sword, but it was too far away to reach.

We're trapped! he thought.

Tom heard the sound of water. He glanced over his shoulder and saw dying grass wreathed in misty vapour. Dank pools lay without a ripple, their edges rimmed with yellow scum. "Elenna, we're at the edge of the Yellow Marshes!"

She wrinkled her nose. Tom could smell the stench of rotten eggs.

"I have an idea for cooling the Red Knight down so that we can fight him," Tom said. "We'll give him a bath in the marshes!"

"Let's do it!" Elenna said, jumping to her feet. "We surrender!" she shouted to the Red Knight as he leapt across the strewn rocks towards them.

"We have no weapons!" Tom called, pointing to where his sword lay lodged against the rock. Elenna unslung her bow from her shoulder and laid it on the ground along with her quiver of arrows. She raised her hands in the air.

The Red Knight broke into a run. Tom willed himself to stand perfectly still. Elenna braced herself beside him. The cursed Knight, raised from the Tombs, rushed forwards, swinging his glowing sword. Tom squinted at the knight's eyes but saw no mercy there.

I hope this works, he thought, as he waited for the knight's attack. *It's our only hope!*

CHAPTER SIX

ACID BATH

The knight raised his sword higher
in both hands as he came closer. Tom
could feel his skin blistering in the
scorching heat as he forced himself
not to flee. The blade hung glittering
above their heads, ready to cleave
them in two.

"Now!" Tom cried.

Tom and Elenna jumped sideways
in opposite directions. The sword

sliced down, whistling in a vertical swipe. Its weight carried the Knight forwards. In a headlong rush, he plunged into the marsh, throwing up a wave of filthy water. Columns of smoke and steam rose from his half-submerged body. The dark waters hissed and bubbled. The knight sank from sight, weighed down by his armour.

Tom stood and helped Elenna to her feet. "Is that the end of him?" she said shakily, stepping away from the bank.

"Let's hope so," said Tom. "Although I'm not sure we can win so easily. I have to find Ferno's scale." He scrambled across to the boulder and retrieved his sword. Pain throbbed in his burned hand as he sheathed the blade. Then he climbed up the slope to search for the Dragon's scale. It was lying, shining and undamaged, on a ridge of rock. Tom gave a sigh of relief as he slid the scale back into his shield. Each talisman was powerful and too important to lose. Still panting from the effort of fighting in the heat, he rejoined Elenna. He gave one last glance at the marshy water. It lay still and oily smooth as though it had never been disturbed by the drowning knight.

Elenna shivered. "I hate this place," she said. "It feels as though everything here is dying. Let's leave and take the Tengi Leaf back to Sana."

Tom nodded. "It'll be good to be back with Storm and Silver too," he said.

He craned his neck to scan the sky. It stretched empty and blue, except for Stonewin's smoke, in every direction. "I'm glad we didn't have to call on Epos and endanger her," he said as they began to walk around the edge of the marshes. This was the first time on this Quest that they hadn't had to call on a Good Beast to help them. Tom couldn't help the nerves that fizzed in his stomach. *This doesn't feel right*, he thought. *Could a knight be defeated that easily?*

Tom remembered the first time

he'd encountered the majestic Beast, Epos. She had helped save Avantia from the volcano's rage by plugging it with rock. In the process, the Flame Bird had lost her life in the cauldron. But she was a Phoenix and had risen again, shining and brave.

"Look!" Elenna pointed, shading her eyes. "Ahead is the burned tree that Sana told us about. We can find the stepping stones beneath it and cross the Marsh on them. It'll be faster than trying to find the stone steps again."

"Good plan," said Tom. The tree's black, twisted limbs hung out over the steaming water. Beneath the branches lay mossy stepping-stones, heading off in different directions through the swamp.

"We must be careful," Elenna said

as she stepped onto the first dark stone. "If we fall into the water, we'll be blind and helpless like Sana."

"Or dead like the Red Knight," said Tom. After a pause, he added, "I wish the knights didn't have to suffer."

"It's the only way to lift the curse," said Elenna.

His friend was right. Like the other knights they'd vanquished, hopefully the Red Knight had returned to his resting place in the Gallery of Tombs. There Malvel's magic could never touch him again.

Tom set each foot down firmly, wary of the slimy moss that coated the stones along their route. When one foot slipped, hot water scalded his toes. Yellow scum coated his boots. Dead grass slapped his knees while horrible fumes swirled into his nostrils and burned his throat. He coughed, bent over, his feet slipping. Behind, he could hear Elenna gagging.

"We can't... We can't make it like this!" she cried between fits of coughing. Her face was pale and she gasped for fresh air.

"In the saddlebag is a spare tunic," Tom panted. "Let's cut it up."

Elenna slung the bag from her shoulder and Tom rummaged inside, pulling out the worn tunic and Elenna's knife. Quickly he ripped the blade through the linen fabric, cutting strips that he and Elenna bound over their faces, covering their mouths and noses.

"This will give us some protection," he said, his voice muffled. Elenna simply nodded, sliding her knife back into the bag. She followed Tom as he took over the lead. It was still hard to breathe but at least now they weren't coughing as much.

"That's better. We'll soon be out…" Tom broke off. He snatched his foot back from the next stone. His heart pounded. Was he imagining things? Had the fumes from the marsh

poisoned his mind? He rubbed his burning eyes and stared hard at the stone. It looked a little rounder than the others, and seemed darker in colour. He thought it had moved when his foot touched it.

Elenna nudged him in the back. "What's wrong?" she asked. "I want to get out of this place!"

"That's not a stone," Tom muttered.

Elenna gasped. The stone moved again, its rounded, mossy surface sending ripples through the dank water. Tom's hand flew to his sword hilt.

Slowly, something rose from the ooze. Shaped like a deformed man, the thing was covered in dark patches of dangling weed and slimy moss. Angry red patches showed where the marsh's toxic waters had burned its flesh.

"It's a Beast," Tom murmured, staring hard.

Taller and taller the Beast rose, three times the height of the Red Knight. He stretched one dripping arm towards Tom, revealing pale webs stretched between each finger.

"Lustor!" Elenna breathed.

Tom recoiled, gripping his sword tighter. The Beast's head, covered in warts and creases like a toad's, bent towards Tom. Lustor's pale eyes swivelled in their sockets. When his mouth gaped open, he revealed stumps of black teeth and bleeding gums.

A sickening stench billowed over Tom. He fought against the retching sensation in his gut. The knight hadn't been killed at all – below

water, he'd transformed into
a Beast!

"He's getting ready to attack!"
Elenna cried. Tom stared at the sac of
skin expanding in the Beast's throat.
It stretched larger, turning almost
translucent. Inside, yellow liquid
bubbled.

"Acid!" Tom shouted, remembering
Sana's description of her encounter
with the Beast. Spinning around,
he jumped from stone to stone,
following Elenna as they tried to find
an escape route out of the marsh.
Tom snatched a glance backwards and
saw the Beast's sac explode, blasting
acid at them, the yellow liquid
splattering into the water all around.
Grass hissed and shrivelled.

A jet of acid hit one side of the
stone on which Tom stood. Before his

shocked eyes, the stone began to melt
away. He leapt onto the next.

Epos, we need help! Tom thought.
But in the next moment, he realized
that he mustn't draw his old friend
into battle with this terrible new
foe. Lustor might kill the Flame Bird
with his acid darts. Then there would
be one less Good Beast to help save

Avantia from Malvel's evil.

We'll fight Lustor by ourselves, Tom thought. *But how can we survive the acid?*

CHAPTER SEVEN

MAROONED!

"We're easy targets here on the stones!" Tom called to Elenna. "Run back to shore. Try to distract Lustor with your arrows. I'll stay here and fight!"

Elenna nodded, gasping for breath. She adjusted the cloth tighter over her nose and began to jump away across the stones. She slipped several times. Tom flinched, afraid that his loyal friend would slide into the terrible waters of the Yellow Marshes.

Tom heard splashing from behind him. He swung around with his sword in his hand. Lustor was wading closer. The poisonous water and smoke didn't seem to affect the Beast at all. His mouth gaped open. His warty head swivelled as he spotted Elenna running along the stones towards the burned tree. Immediately, the sac of acid in his throat expanded again.

"No! Leave her alone!" Tom cried.

But it was too late. A jet of yellow fluid shot across the marsh. Lustor missed and let loose again. Once more the acid failed to reach its target. Again and again, the Beast spat deadly liquid across the marshland. At first Tom thought Elenna was lucky.

She seemed to avoid being hit. But as
stone after stone in front of her was
dissolved, Tom realised he was wrong.
Lustor wasn't aiming for Elenna.

He's cutting off her escape route!

Soon Elenna stood on a single
stone surrounded by the treacherous
marsh. She turned and gave Tom
a desperate glance.

I have to save her, Tom thought as he jumped closer to the Beast and swung his sword, opening up a gash on the Beast's leg, which oozed dark purple fluid. With a savage roar from deep within his warty chest, the Beast turned to face Tom, churning up bubbles of foul gas in the water. The Beast's webbed hands shot out, grasping. Jumping back to another stone, Tom just managed to evade the lumpy fingers. The Beast surged through the water and Tom leapt just ahead on the slippery stones. Once Lustor was able to to grasp the hem of Tom's tunic between the webs of two fingers, but Tom struggled free and staggered forwards, bounding out of reach.

Acid rained around Tom and he lifted his shield for protection. He heard the sizzle across the shield and hoped it wouldn't dissolve. Perhaps the tokens would protect it. A torrent of acid poured off the shield's surface and splashed onto Tom's arm. He yelled in pain as the yellow liquid ate into his flesh. Red burns wrinkled and mottled his skin, just like Sana's.

As he turned to face Lustor, the Beast's rotting mouth opened wider. A thick, long tongue shot towards Tom, dripping with sticky drool.

The tip lashed around Tom's sword like a whip. Lustor used his tongue to wrestle with Tom's sword while Tom tried to hang on to it. With a final twist, the Beast jerked the weapon from Tom and flung it across the marsh. The sword fell into the bubbling liquid with a faint splash and disappeared.

Without a weapon, Tom began to leap along the stones across oozing mud and oily water. Tendrils of steam brushed his cheeks. Behind him the Beast snorted and growled. Tom heard the swoosh of water as Lustor waded in pursuit.

At last, Tom flung himself onto the bank of the swamp. The Beast stopped wading and glared. After a moment, Lustor's stinking mouth stretched wide in an evil grin.

Turning, he began to shoot acid at the stones that Tom had just used to escape. *What's he doing?* Tom wondered. *I'm already out of the marsh.*

Then Tom caught sight of Elenna, trapped in the stinking swamp. Lustor had cut off Tom's route and now the Beast could kill his friend while Tom looked on helplessly.

Tom yanked the strip of linen away from his mouth. He ran along the edge of the marsh. "I'll find a way to you!" he cried to Elenna.

"Hurry!" she yelled back. "I'm trapped!"

Tom clenched his fists, bounding over tussocks of grass and leaping over rocks. Every time he found stepping stones into the marsh, they led in the wrong direction, away from Elenna instead of towards her.

When Tom glanced up, he saw Lustor
wading closer to his friend. The
Beast loomed menacingly above the
dark water. Deadly acid boiled in his

bulging throat sac.

"Elenna, you have the tokens! In the saddlebags!" he shouted. "Find something there to defeat the Beast!"

Elenna quickly fumbled with the buckle of the bag. It was too late. Lustor had reached her. The Beast leant over her, a towering monster of slime and poison. His mouth opened wide.

"No!" Tom shouted in horror.

CHAPTER EIGHT

ONE LAST CHANCE

Tom glanced around desperately
for his sword, hoping to glimpse its
glinting blade in the marsh.

He saw nothing.

"Help, Tom, help!" Elenna cried.
Her voice was drowned out by the
Beast's roar. Elenna was usually so
capable – it hurt Tom to see her so
vulnerable. Lustor's throat-sac grew
larger as the acid welled up inside.

Whoosh!

The moss hanging in the burned
tree blew sideways in a heavy draft
of air. Lustor's misshapen head jerked
upwards with a grunt as a great shape
hurtled from the sky on a scorching
wind.

"Epos!" Tom yelled. A heartbeat
later, his joy at seeing his old friend
turned to dread. Epos would fight
to the death to save either of them.
How could Tom live with himself
if he brought the brave Flame Bird
into danger? Avantia needed all of its
Good Beasts alive.

"Be careful!" Tom called. "Lustor
shoots acid from his throat sac. It
burns anything it touches!"

But he knew Epos couldn't
understand his words. Her huge sail-
like wings churned the air and light

glinted on her dark-gold feathers.
She swooped in low with her fierce,
curved talons outstretched. She
snatched Elenna up into the air.
The phoenix rose up with Elenna

dangling over Lustor's head.

The Evil Beast shot out a webbed hand but Elenna was already too high. He bellowed in fury at losing his prey. For a moment, it looked as though Elenna had been saved.

Fly higher, Epos! Tom willed. *Watch out for Lustor's tongue!*

Elenna kicked her legs but the Beast moved faster. The tip of his sinewy, slimy tongue whipped through the air. It curled around one of Elenna's ankles with the same dreadful grip it had used on Tom's sword. Elenna struggled, kicking and screaming. The Flame Bird thrashed her magnificent wings, straining to break the Beast's grip. Between the bird and the Evil Beast, Elenna writhed. Tom watched from the ground, gripped by desperation. Now two of his loyal

friends were in danger and there
seemed to be nothing he could do.
*I'm on this Quest to save Avantia from
Malvel,* Tom thought, *but I never
wanted my friends to suffer.*

Elenna reached up with her arms,
shifting her bow from her shoulder.
She struggled to seize an arrow. She

somehow managed to notch the shaft. The bowstring curved in her grip.

"Shoot the Beast!" Tom yelled.

The shaft *thrummed* from the bow and the arrowhead grazed Lustor's tongue. With a howl of pain, he released Elenna's ankle. Epos surged higher into the air, her golden eyes blazing. She shrieked with triumph as she circled over the marshes.

But the Beast's throat-sac bulged. A stream of yellow acid shot skywards and Tom groaned in dismay as the liquid splashed on Epos's wing. Smoke trailed from scorched feathers. The noble Flame Bird flapped wildly, lopsided in the air, struggling to stay aloft. Elenna swung from her talons like a doll.

The Phoenix sank lower until

Elenna's feet brushed the tops of the grass and skimmed the dank marsh water.

Are they both going to sink into the poisonous swamp and drown? Tom thought.

Tom began to run along the bank. "Come on, Epos!" he cried as the bird struggled closer. "You can do it!"

The Flame Bird's curved beak opened as she panted with the effort of staying airborne. But with a shudder, she dropped steeply and crashed in a flurry of feathers near the base of the burnt tree. The ground shook beneath the Phoenix's weight. Elenna rolled free and lay limp and stunned. Epos screeched with pain and fury, her talons gouging into the grass. The fire across her wings flared and smoked.

Glancing around, Tom saw Lustor
heave his massive bulk out of the
water and onto the bank. Trailing
weeds and green slime, Lustor
marched towards Tom's fallen friends.
Tom ran, trying to reach them first.

He glimpsed Elenna lurching to her feet, clutching one arm as though it was injured. The Flame Bird too had risen and was conjuring a fireball between her talons. *Yes!* Tom thought with a glimmer of hope. *She'll be able to fight back with the fireball.*

The sparkling ball spun into the air but then sputtered and died. There could be only one explanation: evil magic was being cast to stop her powers.

Tom gasped and ran even harder. While there was blood in his veins, he would bring this to an end. A second fireball glowed beneath Epos's feathers and then extinguished in smoke again. Epos couldn't match Malvel's power.

Tom slid across the final stretch of ground. His heart battered his ribs.

"Where's the saddlebag?" he shouted.

Elenna pointed to where it lay on the ground nearby, dropped when she and Epos had fallen from the sky.

"We have no protection against Lustor!" Elenna cried. "Malvel's magic is growing too strong for us!"

"Don't worry," Tom gasped. "We must have a token in here that I can use."

He fumbled through the contents of the bag, ignoring the searing pain from the acid burn on his arm. Lustor's heavy tread shook the ground. His foul stench assaulted Tom's nostrils.

"Tom!" Elenna screamed, just as Tom's fingers closed over the silver disc. It seemed to be some kind of weapon. One edge of the disc was honed into a razor-sharp blade.

Thoughts raced through Tom's mind. *I've never used this. Will it work against Lustor?* His grip tightened on the disc and he yanked it from the saddlebag as he rose to face the Beast.

Tom turned the disc until the sharp honed edge faced away from Lustor. The Beast was only fifty paces away. He roared, blasting Tom with a hot stench. Acid bubbled in his pale, expanding throat.

Tom gripped the disc, and balanced his weight. *I can only throw this once*, he realised. *If I miss, we're all doomed.*

CHAPTER NINE

THE SILVER DISC

Forty paces… Moss shook in the tree as the Beast's feet pounded across the ground.

Thirty paces… Water quivered in the marsh.

Twenty paces… Elenna swayed beside Tom, still clutching her arm.

As Lustor thundered closer, Tom saw the gleam of triumph in his bulging eyes. The Beast was certain

of victory. Tom inhaled a deep, calming breath. He gripped the token lightly. Then he flung it with all his strength, putting a spin on it with a flick of the wrist. The disc spun through the smoky air, a silver blur as fast as forked lightning.

It sliced into the Beast's throat. Lustor gurgled as a fountain of acid jetted into the sky and rained down upon his body. His mossy, lumpy hide scorched and smoked with a smell like rotting meat. Tom coughed as the sickly stench blew over him. Bellowing in agony, Lustor collapsed to the ground and thrashed wildly. His toad's mouth gaped open and his long tongue flapped like a dying fish. With his webbed hands, Lustor scrabbled at the ground, gouging holes in the soft dirt.

Gradually, the Beast's convulsions became weaker. His bulging eyes closed.

Tom swung away and ran to Elenna, who had slumped back to the ground near Epos. "Are you hurt?" he asked anxiously, bending over her.

"I couldn't reach you any sooner!"

"Oh, Tom, I think my arm is broken from the fall!"

"Let me help you," Tom said, carefully lifting her until she stood up shakily. Tom rolled back the sleeve of her tunic and examined her crooked, swollen arm. "I think you're right," he said.

Elenna grimaced with pain. "Is he dead?"

Tom saw the Beast still lying completely motionless on the banks of the marsh. "Don't worry about that," he said. "You put up a brave struggle. And your arm can be healed with the ruby I won from Skor the Red Stallion."

Elenna nodded, watching as Tom took the jewel from his belt. When Elenna raised her arm, Tom held the crystal near the skin, moving it over the break. Almost at once, the grimace on Elenna's face eased. She tried straightening her arm, and a smile stretched her cheeks. "It's strong again, the bones have knitted back together!" she cried. She turned to look for the Flame Bird. "Is Epos hurt too?"

Tom moved over to the Flame Bird as she flexed the full length of her massive wings. Except for the patch of burned feathers, she seemed unharmed. Her glassy golden eyes stared calmly at Tom. Reaching up, he stroked her shining beak. "Thank you, noble friend, for coming to our aid," he said.

The Flame Bird pealed out a single long note that echoed in Tom's ears. With a couple of powerful wing

beats, she was airborne, lifting high overhead in a dazzle of light. She wobbled once or twice but then became steady and, with a screech of triumph, soared away. Once again, she was the guardian of the volcano, keeping the villages of Avantia safe.

"Look!" Elenna exclaimed, pointing towards the fallen Beast.

Before Tom's shocked gaze, the giant toad seemed to shrink and

crumble in on himself. He became
a misshapen lump like a shovelful of
moss and wet dirt. This too crumbled
and faded to reveal the Red Knight
lying on the ground. His armour,
once fiery and shining, was dented
and rough. The brilliant scarlet colour
had faded to a dull red.

Tom glanced over at him with
a troubled frown. "Surely he can't
be alive?"

CHAPTER TEN

TWO WARNINGS

"Don't go too close!" Elenna warned
as she followed Tom over to the
knight.

"He's breathing, but only just,"
Tom said, watching the shallow rise
and fall of the armour plates on the
knight's chest. The visor had fallen
open and the knight's haggard face
lay exposed to the sunlight. His eyes
swivelled at Tom's approach and

he gave a weak smile.

"Although I have tried to kill you, now I must thank you." The knight's voice was weary and hoarse. "You succeeded in freeing me from Malvel's curse."

Tom and Elenna leant close, straining to hear the knight's words. "I remember once, long ago, how I helped my Master of the Beasts

to conquer Lustor. The Beast was a terrifying foe. Victory over him was our greatest achievement."

"I would have liked to meet your Master," Tom said.

"Tanner was one of the bravest young men I knew, but you are a worthy successor to him."

Elenna started with surprise and Tom flushed. "I am not Master of the Beasts, sir," he explained. "That is the position held by Taladon, my father."

The knight gave a mysterious smile. "Perhaps you are not Master yet."

"Not yet?" Tom echoed doubtfully. Could the knight foretell the future? Tom opened his mouth to speak but the knight's face contorted in a grimace.

"Are you in pain?" Tom asked. He leant closer, supporting the Red

Knight's head and shoulders in his arms. The warrior's features blurred and shifted. What was happening? Suddenly Tom found himself looking into the cruel face of Malvel. Tom recoiled as the Evil Wizard grinned.

"Ah, Tom," he said. "How hard you are fighting in Avantia! But what a useless endeavour! Soon I shall return. By then, you and Elenna will be dead. Three knights remain from the Gallery of Tombs for you to face. One of them will take your life, I promise!"

"While there's blood in my veins, I will fight your twisted Beasts!" Tom cried. "If you take a step back in Avantia, I will be waiting for you!"

Malvel's face faded as Tom spoke and the knight grew lighter in Tom's arms until he weighed less than a sheaf of hay. His skin turned waxy and his armour faded. In only a few heartbeats, Tom's arms were empty.

"Where has he gone?" Elenna asked in wonder.

"Tom, you have done well," said a familiar voice behind them. He and Elenna spun around to see an image of Aduro standing beneath the burned tree. The good wizard smiled, his eyes shining with kindness.

"Do not worry about the Red Knight," Aduro said. "He has returned to the Gallery of Tombs where he belongs. He has earned his rest for eternity."

The wizard's glance ran over Elenna's torn sleeve and scratched face, then over Tom's burned arm. "Acid has scalded you," he said. "Can you carry on?"

Tom clambered to his feet and straightened his back. "I'll never desert the Quest," he said, his chin lifted and his eyes steady.

"And neither will I!" said Elenna, standing at Tom's shoulder.

"That is well spoken. Tom, you will need your sword," Aduro responded. He stretched his hand towards the stagnant waters of the Yellow Marshes. For a moment the water lay dark and flat. Then a ripple stirred. With a sudden flash, the sword broke the surface. It soared upwards through the rising steam, turning end over end. Water streamed off its glittering blade. The hilt flipped into Aduro's waiting grasp and the wizard held it out to Tom. After wiping the blade clean on the grass, Tom slid it into the sheath at his belt. It was good

to feel the sword's familiar weight
hanging at his side.

"Look at Portos!" Elenna said with
a laugh.

The little swallow fluttered around
Aduro's shoulders, trying to land
there. Instead, the bird kept flying
right through the vision of the
Wizard.

"Portos reminds me that Sana

needs her Tengi Leaf," Tom said. "Once she is healed, we will be free to face Malvel's next Beast."

Aduro's face folded into grim lines of concern. "I can feel Malvel's power growing stronger each day," he warned. "You have defeated three cursed knights but three more enemies await you. Don't underestimate the battles to come. Your strength will be sorely tested."

With this warning, the Wizard faded from sight. Portos fluttered, chirruping, around Tom's head. "Come on," Tom said to Elenna. "Let's return to the north road and find Storm and Silver."

"We'll need them in the battles that lie ahead," Elenna said.

Together they strode through the marshes on the remaining stones.

As soon as they were on the road again, Tom felt courage swell in his heart. This stage of his Quest was over, but another stage waited.

And we'll be ready! he promised himself. *I'll do whatever it takes to save Avantia.*

Join Tom on the next stage
of the Beast Quest when he meets

VOLTREX
THE TWO-HEADED
OCTOPUS

Win an exclusive
Beast Quest T-shirt and goody bag!

Tom has battled many fearsome Beasts and we want to know
which one is your favourite! Send us a drawing or painting of
your favourite Beast and tell us in 30 words why you think
it's the best.

Each month we will select **three** winners to receive
a Beast Quest T-shirt and goody bag!

Send your entry on a postcard to
BEAST QUEST COMPETITION
Orchard Books, 338 Euston Road, London NW1 3BH.

Australian readers should email:
childrens.books@hachette.com.au

New Zealand readers should write to:
Beast Quest Competition, 4 Whetu Place, Mairangi Bay,
Auckland NZ, or email: childrensbooks@hachette.co.nz

**Don't forget to include your name and address.
Only one entry per child.**

Good luck!

Join the Quest,
Join the Tribe

www.beastquest.co.uk

Have you checked out the Beast Quest website?
It's the place to go for games, downloads, activities,
sneak previews and lots of fun!

You can read all about your favourite Beasts, download free screensavers and desktop wallpapers for
your computer, and even challenge your friends
to a Beast Tournament.

Sign up to the newsletter at www.beastquest.co.uk
to receive exclusive extra content and the opportunity to enter special members-only competitions.
We'll send you up-to-date info on all the Beast
Quest books, including the next exciting series
which features six brand-new Beasts!

Get 30% off all Beast Quest Books at www.beastquest.co.uk
Enter the code BEAST at the checkout.

All books priced at £4.99,
special bumper editions
priced at £5.99.

Orchard Books are available from all good bookshops, or can
be ordered from our website: www.orchardbooks.co.uk,
or telephone 01235 827702, or fax 01235 8227703.

Beast Quest ®

Series 10: MASTER OF THE BEASTS
COLLECT THEM ALL!

An old enemy has come back to haunt Tom –
and unleash six awesome new Beasts!

NOCTILA THE DEATH OWL

978 1 40831 518 7

SHAMANI THE RAGING FLAME

978 1 40831 519 4

LUSTOR THE ACID DART

978 1 40831 520 0

VOLTREX THE TWO-HEADED OCTOPUS

978 1 40831 521 7

TECTON THE ARMOURED GIANT

978 1 40831 522 4

DOOMSKULL THE KING OF FEAR

978 1 40831 523 1

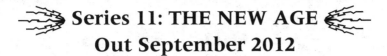

Series 11: THE NEW AGE
Out September 2012

Meet six terrifying new Beasts!

Elko Lord of the Sea
Tarrok the Blood Spike
Brutus the Hound of Horror
Flaymar the Scorched Blaze
Serpio the Slithering Shadow
Tauron the Pounding Fury

**Watch out for the next
Special Bumper
Edition
OUT OCT 2012!**

SPECIAL BUMPER EDITION!

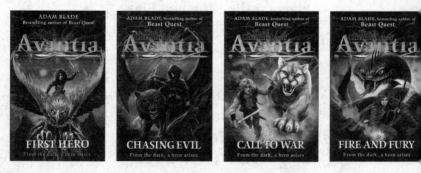